For THAT GOOD MOTHER-IN-LAW
M.W.

First U.S. edition 1990

First published in 1989 in Great Britain by
Walker Books Ltd., London
Library of Congress Catalog Card Number 89-84974
10 9 8 7 6 5 4 3 2 1
Joy Street Books are published by
Little, Brown and Company (Inc.)
Printed in Italy

AMY SAID

Written by Martin Waddell
Illustrated by Charlotte Voake

Little, Brown and Company
Boston Toronto London

When Amy and I stayed with Gran,

I wanted to bounce on my bed.

Amy said I could!

I just bounced a bit,

then a bit more,

then a bit more.

Then I fell off the bed.   And Amy said . . .

we could *swing* instead.

"Gran's curtains are fun,"
Amy said.

And she swung

and she crashed

and she bashed Gran's chair!

It was all *my* fault, Amy said.

Gran gave us hot dogs and beans for lunch.

"Max likes hot dogs and beans," Amy said.

So I gave mine to Max.

And Max made a mess

of them

all over the floor.

Amy said perhaps Gran wouldn't see

because Gran was making me . . .

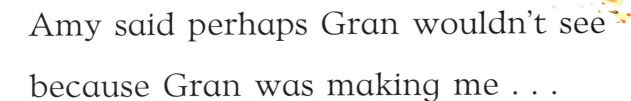

a Monster Head!

Amy said it was a Green Gobbler.

And Amy drew pictures

in green and red

to say thank you to Gran

for making my head.

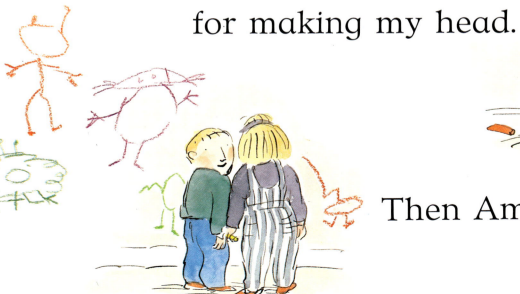

Then Amy said,

"The walls need painting now!"

So I painted them green

like my Monster Head.

And Max came

and did it *again*.

Then Amy said . . .

we should give some milk to Gran's cat

for being so good and for

not making messes like Max.

But as well as the milk,

Gran's cat

took Gran's fish.

And Amy said . . .

we should pick

Gran some flowers

in case she was mad.

So we picked ALL of the flowers

in Gran's garden.

I don't think she was mad

because . . .

she gave us a party

with cake and buns

and ice cream for everyone.

And Amy said,

"Let's play!"

So we did.

Then our friends went home
and Amy and I went to help
Gran in her garden.

Amy dug and dug . . .

until she went

SPLOSH!

When Gran saw us

she put us both in the bathtub.

We splashed just a bit, but the water

went on the floor.

And Gran said . . .

"That's enough! NO MORE!"

Then she helped us get dry and she said,

"*Please* try to be good!"

And Amy said

that we would . . .

and we were.